To: Lauren

Love xoxo Dad
9/8/97

A KID'S GUIDE TO THE MOON

by Glenn Taylor

Illustrated by Nathan Y. Jarvis

Published by Capstone Press, Inc.

Distributed By

CP CHILDRENS PRESS®

CHICAGO

CIP

LIBRARY OF CONGRESS CATALOGING IN PUBLICATION DATA

Taylor, Glenn.
A kid's guide to living on the moon / by Glenn Taylor.
p. cm.-- (Star shows)
Summary: Danny and Cathy compile a travel book for visitors to
the moon, describing the lunar phases, craters, and orbit, the Apollo
11 landing, and future activities at a lunar colony.

ISBN 1-56065-015-X

1. Moon--Juvenile literature. 2. Moon--Exploration--Juvenile
literature. [1. Moon. 2. Moon--Exploration.] I. Title. II. Series.
QB582.T385 1989
629.45'4--dc20   89-25190 CIP AC

Designed by Nathan Y. Jarvis & Associates, Inc.

Capstone Press

Box 669, Mankato, MN, U.S.A. 56001

CONTENTS

THE MOON WATCHERS

THIS IS THE STORY of how Danny and Cathy started out doing their homework and ended up on the moon.

It all began when they did a report on the moon in school. They wanted to observe something in nature. They chose the moon.

The first night, they were ready. They had flashlights, hot chocolate, warm clothes, clipboards, binoculars, and a watch. Only one thing was missing: the moon! They went out each night after that. Still no moon. Then, one evening, with the glow of the sun still in the sky, they saw the moon. It was a thin bright sliver of light in the west. They wrote down on their clipboard what time it was and where in the sky they saw it. Cathy drew a picture of it.

They looked in a book and found out why they hadn't seen the moon before. It was something called the "New Moon."

Cathy and Danny found out that when the moon is on the side of the Earth in daylight, it is between the Earth and the sun. The sun lights up the side of the moon people can't see. The side facing Earth is completely dark. This is called the **New Moon**.

A day or two after the New Moon, people on Earth see the moon as a thin sliver in the shape of a crescent. That's because a small part of the half that is lighted by the sun is visible. The small sliver that Cathy and Danny finally saw was the **Crescent Moon**.

The next evening, Danny and Cathy went outside at the same time they did before.

"There it is," Danny said. "I'll write down the time."

Cathy drew another picture of the moon over the trees. "It's higher than it was yesterday," she said. "And it's a little further to the east." Each evening they wrote down what they saw and drew a picture. They put it all into a notebook.

"Look at these drawings," Cathy said one evening. "You can see how every night the moon moves further to the east. And every night we can see more of it." Cathy and Danny looked in another book to find out why.

About a week after the New Moon, half of the side facing Earth is lit. This is called **First Quarter**. The portion of the moon that is lit is one quarter of its total surface. In other words, half of the half that is lighted by the sun is visible to people on Earth.

More of the moon showed each evening. They began to notice dark areas against the bright surface features. They also noticed that the dark areas did not move.

"I guess that means that the moon doesn't turn at all," Danny said.

"But wait," Cathy said. "The moon goes around the Earth. It must turn. It just turns very slowly. Maybe it turns around once every time it goes around Earth. Then the same side would always face Earth." They looked it up in a book. Cathy was right. The moon turns around once in about 29 and a half days. It takes about that long for it to go once around the Earth. That's why we see only one side of the moon from the Earth.

Every night more of the side facing the sun was visible. About a week after the First Quarter and two weeks after the New Moon, the Earth was between the moon and the sun.

The entire half of the moon lit by the sun was visible from the Earth. This is called the **Full Moon**.

For several evenings after that, Cathy and Danny couldn't find the moon. They wondered where it had gone. Then they realized that it was on the other side of the Earth!

Their parents let them stay up late one night. Sure enough, the moon finally did appear. Cathy and Danny couldn't stay up late enough to see the moon rise a few days past Full Moon. But they could see the moon in the morning. They wrote the time in their notebook and drew more pictures.

"Now it's getting smaller each day," Danny said.

"I guess that's because it's getting around to the day side of Earth," Cathy answered. "So the moon is between the Earth and the sun."

Cathy wrote in her notebook. "If you are looking for the moon, remember: It rises about an hour later each night. The night of the Full Moon, it rises at the same time the sun sets. After that, you must stay up later and later every night to see the moon."

About a week after the Full Moon, the moon was at **Last Quarter**. It had moved to the side of the Earth. Only half of the side facing the Earth was lit. This is called the Last Quarter since the portion of the moon that can be seen from the Earth is one quarter of the total surface of the moon.

Finally, they could no longer see the moon. It was directly between the Earth and the sun. The dark half faced the Earth. It was New Moon again.

Danny wrote in his notebook. "It takes about one week to go from the New Moon to the First Quarter. Then about one more week to get to the Full Moon. Then about one more week to get to the Last Quarter. And finally, about one more week to get back to New Moon. The whole thing takes a little over a month."

Danny and Cathy drew a diagram of the moon at different phases. They drew in the positions of the sun and the Earth. They watched the moon again. This time they used a pair of binoculars. They made a map of the moon and labeled the dark areas and the mountain ranges. Finally, they made a cover. They were done. The title read, "A Kid's Guide to the Moon."

THE ADVENTURE BEGINS

At school the next day, Cathy and Danny proudly showed "A Kid's Guide to the Moon" to their teacher. She was so impressed, she showed their work to the principal. The principal was so impressed, she sent it off to **NASA**, the National Aeronautics and Space Administration. NASA invited Cathy and Danny for a tour of the space museum.

At the space museum, Danny and Cathy saw Saturn V, the rocket that carried the first humans to the moon. Later in the tour, they climbed into an early spacecraft. Their guide, Ms. Futuro, asked them an interesting question.

"Would you like to go to the moon someday?" she said.

"Oh yes," Cathy answered.

"Are you kidding?" Danny asked. "You bet I would. That would be fantastic."

"As you probably know," Ms. Futuro said, "kids were not allowed in space until recently. There were problems with loss of bone material and other changes. That was fine for adults, but it could have hurt kids. But now, with some new treatments, kids are cleared for space. There are already several kids living at the colony on the moon. More will be moving there soon. NASA would like somebody to write a guide to the moon for those kids. They've seen your work. They want you to do it. They want you to expand 'A Kid's Guide to the Moon' and tell kids what it's like to live on the moon. Are you interested?"

Cathy and Danny could hardly believe their ears. They were so surprised, they just stared at each other. Ms. Futuro went on.

"You'll have to go to the moon yourselves, of course. Then you can write about your experiences for other kids. Talk it over with your parents and let me know."

KIDS IN SPACE

Cathy and Danny didn't have any trouble deciding. Several months later, they found themselves halfway to the moon aboard the lunar transfer rocket, Spacefarer. Through a large viewport, they watched the Earth get smaller each hour. Ms. Futuro tried to keep up with all their questions. They wrote the answers in their notebooks for A Kid's Guide to the Moon.

"Why are there so many **craters** on the moon and none on Earth?" Cathy asked. "And why are there animals and plants on Earth and none on the moon? And why is Earth blue and white and brown and green and the moon just gray?"

"Whoa," said Ms. Futuro, "one question at a time. Let's start with your question about why Earth is alive with plants and animals and air and life and the moon is gray and barren. Think about it. What is different about the moon?"

"There's no air on the moon," said Danny. "Things can't grow and live without air."

"That's right," said Ms. Futuro. "And why doesn't the moon have any air? This is tricky, so think about it a moment." Danny and Cathy were quiet, thinking.

"The Earth is bigger than the moon," said Cathy.

"You're on to something there," said Ms. Futuro. "The answer has to do with **gravity**, that amazing property of all **matter** that causes it to attract and to be attracted by all other matter. The moon and the Earth both have gravity, of course, but which has more?"

"Earth has more," said Cathy. "It's bigger than the moon."

"That's right," said Ms. Futuro. "The diameter of the moon is only about one fourth that of the Earth. Because of what it is made of, and its smaller size, it has only about one sixth the gravity of Earth. The weaker gravity of the moon was not strong enough to hold an atmosphere. So there's no air on the moon. Now, what about your other question?"

"You mean about the craters?" asked Cathy.

"Right. Why are there all those craters on the moon and hardly any on Earth?"

Cathy gazed at the blue and white Earth against the black of space. "Water," she shouted. "Earth has water and water changes things. The moon and the Earth probably both got bashed by thousands and thousands of rocks floating in space when the solar system was new. The moon had no air, no water. There was nothing to wipe away the craters that the **meteorites** left. Earth has rain and wind and snow and ice. Did I get it right?"

"Nice going, Cathy," said Ms. Futuro. "You have most of the answer. Earth is one of the most active planets in the solar system. Earthquakes and volcanoes as well as erosion from wind and rain continually change the surface. That's why the face of the Earth changes and the moon remains the same."

"You said that Earth had hardly any craters," said Danny. "Do you mean it does have some craters?"

"That's right," said Ms. Futuro. "Scientists have identified several features that they believe may have been caused by meteorites striking the Earth."

As Spacefarer approached the moon, Danny and Cathy studied the cratered surface.

"Look," said Cathy. "Those dark patches we could see when we looked at the moon from the Earth are the flat places. All the mountains and the high places are lighter."

"And look at all those craters," said Danny. "They're all different sizes! And look at that light-colored stuff around that big crater. It looks like it got splattered out when a meteorite hit."

"The edges of the craters all look so sharp," said Cathy. "And the mountains look really rough."

"And it all looks gray," added Danny. They got out the map they had made from watching the moon from the Earth. They recognized the familiar dark plains and light highlands.

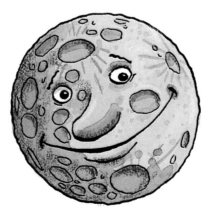

HOW DID THE MOON GET LIKE THIS?

The journey to the moon took about three days. As Spacefarer went into lunar **orbit**, they could clearly see details on the moon's surface. The Spacefarer skimmed over the gray hills, gray mountains, and gray plains. Craters, thousands of them in all sizes, filled their field of view.

"How did the moon get like this?" Danny asked.

"No one is sure how the moon formed," Ms. Futuro answered. "One idea is that it was a part of the Earth that broke away. Another idea is that the moon formed from debris that surrounded the sun. The part of the story that scientists are still studying began about four-and-a-half billion years ago. The moon was a ball of hot molten rock. Heavier elements, such as iron, sank deep below the surface.

Lighter materials, such as aluminum and calcium, remained near the top. As the surface cooled, the lighter materials formed the crust.

"Four billion years ago, rocks ranging in size from grains of sand to houses swarmed in the vast spaces between the newly forming planets. As the planets and their moons moved through space, the rocks crashed into them. That's what made all the craters on the moon.

"One particularly huge meteorite, perhaps as large as 100 kilometers across (about 60 miles), slammed into the moon about four billion years ago. The impact broke the crust and molten lava flowed out, flooding the low-lying plains. These dark areas can be seen from the Earth without telescopes. People on Earth named them '**Maria**' (MAHR-i-a). 'Maria' is Latin for 'seas.' The far side of the moon, the side that always faces away from the Earth, has only a few small dark low-lying areas. This may be because the crust on the far side is thicker than the crust on the near side."

Spacefarer orbited the moon once, then descended toward the surface. Cathy and Danny watched as the hills and craters grew closer. The spacecraft fired its rockets to slow the descent. Soon they saw a jumble of buildings with curved roofs and a landing pad.

"I can't believe we're really here on the moon," Cathy said as the Spacefarer touched down.

"I can't wait to get out there and jump around on the craters," Danny said.

But Cathy and Danny were disappointed. They were told to stay aboard Spacefarer for an important briefing. A woman and a man, both dressed in blue jumpsuits, entered the cabin.

WELCOME TO THE MOON

"Welcome to the moon," said the woman. She introduced herself as the Safety Officer for the colony. "Sorry to delay you after your long trip but there are just a few things you need to know before we turn you loose. We'll keep this as brief as possible. You'll be given other instructions on space suits, how to use the airlocks, how to get supplies, and so on. But for now, you need to know a few important things to keep you out of trouble. We call them the Seven Things You Must Never Do on the Moon."

"First of all, you must *never open any windows* here on the moon. There is air inside the buildings and no air outside. If you forget and open a window, all the air will rush out and you will die. The windows have levers that open in an emergency, so be careful and do not touch them.

"The second thing you must never do on the moon is *jump when you're inside*. You may have already noticed how light you feel. The gravity on the moon is only one sixth that on the Earth. You weigh only one sixth what you do on Earth. You can jump six times higher here than on Earth. As you may have noticed, our ceilings are not six times higher here than on Earth. Outside, fine. You can jump all you like. We ask that you do not jump over any buildings, however, as you may meet someone jumping from the other side.

"Third, *no baths*. Showers only. Water is scarce here on the moon and we do not waste it. All waste water is collected, filtered, and recycled. We also get some water from fuel cells used to generate our electrical power. Please conserve water.

"The fourth rule is *never go outside alone*. We use the buddy system here. If you're going out, be sure that people know where you're going and how long you'll be gone. If you have any problems, call the base and we'll send someone out to help you.

"Number Five seems obvious, but you never know. *Never go outside without your spacesuit*. Have the suit maintenance crew check your suit each time for leaks and be sure the unit is fully charged. Watch the life support monitors on your spacesuit. Come back before your air is gone. You will get a complete space suit briefing later.

"Rule Number Six has to do with touching valves and switches: Don't! *Don't open or close any valve or switch* unless you know what you're doing. The valves and switches control airflow to the buildings and to scrubbers that remove carbon dioxide. Air is brought here from Earth. Oxygen is either brought from the Earth or made from green plants. We lose some air from the airlocks. We can't afford to lose any through accidents or carelessness, so be careful.

"And finally, Rule Number Seven: when you drive the lunar rovers, do not, I repeat, *do not drive faster than 15 kilometers per hour!* That's 11 miles per hour. If you were to exceed this speed limit and you struck a bump, the low lunar gravity would allow the rover to leave the ground. And who knows where or when you'd come down again."

The Safety Officer finished. She introduced the man beside her as the Science Officer.

WHAT'S THERE TO DO
ON THE MOON?

The Science Officer stepped forward. "You're probably wondering, what's there to do on the moon? The answer is, plenty. After you get settled in, you'll report to the ward room. There we'll get you fitted for your space suit. Once you've been checked out, the other kids will show you some crazy things you can do here on the moon. You wouldn't even <u>think</u> of doing them on Earth.

"We also have exciting trips for you. You might assist the scientists with their studies. Or you might go on a field trip to collect rock samples for the lunar geology people. We hope to find something we call 'orange soil' near areas of ancient volcanic activity. People called vulcanologists back on Earth will study them. We're also planning a field trip some time next month to the seismic station. There, scientists record 'moonquakes.'

24

"You may want to join our astronomy club. Since the moon rotates so slowly, 'daytime' here is about two weeks long. That makes the moon a great place for studying the sun. The moon is also a great place for studying the **solar wind.** The solar wind is a stream of high speed particles that the sun casts off. After the sun sets, we have a two-week long 'nighttime.' That's a great time to look at stars, planets, galaxies, nebulas, and comets. We can also photograph them. And we never have to worry about the weather. There isn't any!

"If you like traveling, you can go on trips to other parts of the moon. You can explore the mountain ranges, rifts, and craters. You may also wish to visit places where some of the first spacecraft from Earth landed.

"We also do many of the same things you do on Earth: sports, art, music, dance, games, gymnastics, and theater. But here on the moon, each of these is full of new possibilities. I hope you all brought good imaginations."

"When do we get to go outside?" Danny asked.

"As soon as you've had your spacesuit briefing and been fitted with your suit," replied the Science Officer with a grin.

LIVING IN A SPACE SUIT

Danny and Cathy followed Ms. Futuro to the ward room. They were startled to see a row of spacekids about their size. Their mirrored visors looked like shiny goldfish bowls and hid their faces. Then Cathy and Danny realized that these were empty space suits. They laughed.

"Are you two ready for your first lesson on living inside a space suit?" Ms. Futuro asked. Danny and Cathy nodded.

Ms. Futuro handed each of them what looked like a pile of clear spaghetti. "What's all this stuff?" Danny asked.

"Underwear," replied Ms. Futuro. "It goes on over your regular underwear. Let me ask you some questions while I measure you. Why do we need to wear spacesuits on the moon?"

Cathy and Danny tried to remember the

briefings they'd had on Earth. "Protection?" answered Danny timidly.

"Okay, protection from what?" asked Ms. Futuro.

Cathy thought hard. What was so bad about the moon that you had to wear a spacesuit? Maybe it was too cold. "The cold," said Cathy.

Danny was also thinking. Maybe it was the sun that he needed protection from. It sure felt hot where the sun shone. "The heat," said Danny.

Ms. Futuro laughed. "Guess what. You're both right. It's hot where the sun shines and cold in the shade. Objects in the sunlight are much too hot to touch. And objects in the shade are very cold. So one purpose for wearing a spacesuit is for protection from heat and cold. Your suit will keep you at just the right temperature. Your body gives off heat, too. So the suit must adjust for that. Here, try this on." Ms. Futuro handed them each a pile of cloth with plastic tubing woven into it.

"Thanks," Danny and Cathy said, without much enthusiasm.

"What does this stuff do?" asked Cathy.

"This stuff is underwear," said Ms. Futuro. "It's made of tiny tubes that carry water from your life support back pack. The water carries away heat from hot places and warms cold places inside the suit. It helps keep you comfortable. Think of it as your own indoor plumbing."

Cathy and Danny slipped easily into the strange suits made of tiny tubes.

"What else do you need a spacesuit for here on the moon?" asked Ms. Futuro.

"Well, there's no air on the moon," said Danny. "I need air to breathe."

"Right," said Ms. Futuro. "Your back pack contains your life support systems. Your body needs oxygen to stay alive. It also needs to get rid of carbon dioxide. Look inside here. This cylinder holds oxygen for you to breathe. The air you breathe out is recirculated and the carbon dioxide is scrubbed out. As you use up the oxygen, more is added to the air you breathe. And there's something else about air that you may not be aware of."

"On the surface of the Earth, pressure pushes on your body. The pressure is caused by the weight of the air in the atmosphere. We don't normally think of air as having weight but it does. That pressure is about 15 pounds on every square inch of your body. You don't feel it because your body is made of mostly

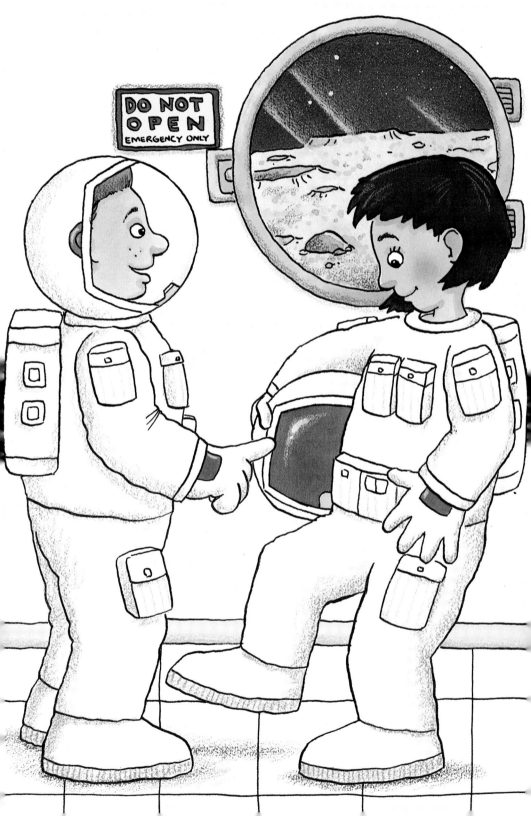

liquids and solids. But you can feel changes in pressure, like when your ears pop in an airplane." Ms. Futuro opened the refrigerator and took out a bottle of soda.

"Is that for me?" Cathy asked, suddenly thirsty.

"You can both have some when we're done. This bottle of soda is going to help me explain why you need a spacesuit here on the moon. Look at this soda. It's clear. Do you see any bubbles of gas in it?"

Cathy and Danny both shook their heads.

"Actually, it does have gas in it but you can't see it. The gas is dissolved in the soda. It stays dissolved in the soda because the soda is put into the bottle under pressure." Ms. Futuro pulled out a bottle opener and snapped the cap off.

"Now I see bubbles," said Cathy.

"Right. We have removed the pressure. The gas, which was dissolved in the soda, formed bubbles."

"But what does this have to do with spacesuits?" asked Cathy.

"Your body has gas dissolved inside it, too, just like the soda. Your body needs pressure to keep the gas dissolved. If the pressure is suddenly taken away, bubbles of gas would form inside your body and that..."

"...doesn't sound very good to me," said Cathy.

"It's not," said Ms. Futuro. "And for that reason, you must be careful not to tear the suit. The suit has seals that keep in the pressure. The outside is made of tough materials, but you must still be careful. Take your time checking out each seal as you suit up."

"Why don't they just put a lot of extra pressure inside the suit so that if it leaked, you would still have enough pressure inside?" asked Danny.

"That's a good question. Actually, they put in less pressure than you are used to on Earth. I see you frowning. Let me ask you this: have you ever noticed that when you blow up a balloon the more you inflate it the stiffer it gets? Your spacesuit is the same as the balloon. If we put too much pressure inside, the arms and legs would be too stiff. You wouldn't be able to bend them. By using a lower pressure, the suit is more flexible. You may still get tired. You are constantly bending your arms and legs against the pressure that wants to keep the arms and legs straight."

"When can we go outside?" Cathy asked.

"Soon. I just need two more measurements and I'll put your suits together." Ms. Futuro finished and disappeared around a corner. She returned a moment later with two boxes labeled "Lunar Surface Exposure Suit: Weight 100 pounds."

"100 pounds!" cried Danny, "I can't lift 100 pounds!"

Ms. Futuro smiled. "100 pounds is what the suit weighs on Earth. Remember, the moon has only about one sixth as much gravity. So your suits only weigh about one sixth of 100 pounds or about 17 pounds. Think you can handle that?"

"I guess so," said Danny.

Ms. Futuro unpacked the strange looking piles of stiff white wrinkled arms and legs from the boxes. She attached the arms and legs to the torso of the suit with locking rings and seals. Cathy reached out and felt the suit.

"Why is this so thick and stiff?" she asked.

"More protection," said Ms. Futuro. "We don't like to talk about it, but we do get occasional showers here on the moon."

"Showers! You mean it rains here?" asked Cathy.

"No, of course not," laughed Ms. Futuro.

32

"It never rains on the moon. The showers we get are **micrometeor** showers. You don't have to worry about micrometeors on Earth. Earth's atmosphere, all that thick air that surrounds the Earth, protects you from them. The micrometeors we worry about are smaller than grains of sand."

"But sand can't hurt you," said Cathy.

"It can if it is traveling at 40,000 kilometers per hour. That's about 25,000 miles per hour! The outer layer of the spacesuit has to be tough. We don't want any holes in our pressure suit — not even tiny ones. The outer part of the spacesuit is like a bullet-proof vest." Ms. Futuro opened a cabinet and lifted out two white helmets with shiny gold visors. "Here, try these on. How does that feel?" asked Ms. Futuro over the helmet radio.

"Fine," said Danny. "Why is this visor tinted? Is it like sunglasses?"

"The sun is bright," said Ms. Futuro. "We do need some light protection. But more important, that visor is coated with special materials. They prevent harmful rays from the sun from blinding you. On the Earth, the atmosphere filters out most of the really harmful rays from the sun. There is no protection here on the moon."

"Why are we talking over a radio?"

"Remember, there is no air outside," Ms. Futuro said. "Sound can't travel without air. Well, do you two think you are ready to go outside?"

Ms. Futuro helped Cathy and Danny into their suits. She carefully checked each fitting. When Danny and Cathy were dressed, Ms. Futuro got into her own suit.

GOING OUTSIDE FOR THE FIRST TIME

"Are you ready?" she asked. Cathy and Danny both nodded. They heard each other breathing over the radios. "Okay, step over here to the airlock," said Ms. Futuro. "Remember, once you are outside, watch your balance. In this light gravity, it's easy to fall over on your face. And please don't go jumping over the buildings yet."

The airlock door swung open and they stepped inside. The green light inside went off and the yellow light came on. The air rushed out of the lock in a muffled hiss. As the air pressure dropped, their suits stiffened. It suddenly got quiet. They noticed that the red light was on. There was no air in the lock. Ms. Futuro turned the wheel on the outer door and it swung open.

Danny and Cathy stepped carefully out onto a metal grid. The gray lunar soil was covered with footprints. They stepped out onto the moon. It felt like walking on moist sand.

"Can you hear me?" asked Ms. Futuro. Danny and Cathy did not answer. They were too busy staring off across the gray lunar landscape. "It's okay, don't be afraid. Let's join the others," said Ms. Futuro, pointing toward a group of kids bouncing by.

Danny felt top-heavy. He concentrated on his balance. Cathy tried an awkward step, then another. Their suits were stiff. It took some effort to bend their arms and legs. They watched the other kids for a moment. Everyone was hopping about like kangaroos. Finally, they let their arms hang and tried hopping. That worked fine. Soon they were bounding along in a loping gallop across the flat area between the buildings.

Off across the compound they went with the other bubble-headed kids. The group was headed for the launch and landing area. Something was going on. The Spacefarer was gone. Cathy and Danny bounded along toward the pad. A group of kids was watching a space-suited skateboarder swoop around the smooth curved sides of the blast deflectors. The rider

seemed to move in slow motion. At the lip he did two complete flips before landing softly back on the slope.

"I'm glad we brought our skateboards," Cathy said.

At a basketball court nearby, players their size flew high above the ground. They gracefully slam-dunked the ball.

"The moon is going to be a fun place," Danny said.

In the shade of a storage shed they saw several small children. They appeared to be sticking lumps of clay onto someone's suit. "What are they doing?" asked Danny.

"Oh that," said Ms. Futuro. That's cookie dough. The kids stick it on their suits, then stand in the sunlight for a while to bake the cookies."

"Does it work?" asked Cathy.

"Not very well," replied Ms. Futuro. "By the time they get them inside to eat, they're frozen solid."

Talking about cookies reminded Cathy and Danny that they were hungry. They went back inside the space station for some lunch.

A VISIT TO AN HISTORIC SITE

Afterward, they got suited up in their spacesuits again. They joined Ms. Futuro and the others who had just arrived on the moon. They all climbed aboard a small transport rocket. It took them across the moon to an area known as the Sea of Tranquility.

"Today, we'll be visiting the historic site where two men from the Earth first set foot on the moon," Ms. Futuro told them. "It was in July, 1969.

"The three astronauts on that mission were Neil Armstrong, Edwin Aldrin, and Michael Collins. Collins remained in orbit around the moon in the command module, named Columbia. Armstrong and Aldrin descended to the surface in the lunar module, named Eagle. They were running low on fuel. The astronauts had to fly the rocket over a boulder field to find a smooth place to land.

Then their rocket began kicking up dust on the surface. On Earth, everyone at mission control and everyone watching on television held their breath. The astronauts watched as the shadow of their spacecraft on the ground came closer. Sensors on the landing pads touched the surface and the astronauts radioed they were shutting down the engines. 'We copy you down!' came the worried call from Earth. Then came the first radio transmission from the astronauts on the surface of the moon: 'Tranquility Base here. The Eagle has landed'."

Danny and Cathy looked out at the lifeless gray expanse of the moon. They wondered what it must have been like for the first astronauts and for the people back on Earth. They both quietly got out their notebooks. They wrote their feelings for the Kid's Guide to the Moon.

"Neil Armstrong was the first one to step onto the surface of the moon," Ms. Futuro continued. "He backed down the ladder and jumped. Millions of people on Earth watched the pictures coming live. Armstrong's first words were, 'That's one small step for man, one giant leap for mankind'."

The transport glided over hills and craters and out over a smooth dark gray plain.

Small boulders and craters covered the ground. The transport touched down softly and everyone jumped to the moon's gray surface. They followed the guide over a track covered with bootprints. At the top of a slight rise everyone stopped at a railing.

A large gold-covered contraption with legs sat like a giant insect. "The Lunar Module is still there," said Ms. Futuro. "When the astronauts left, only the top part of the ship, the Lunar Ascent Module, went up. The bottom part stayed here and acted as a launch pad."

"The flag looks like the wind is blowing it," said Danny.

"It does, doesn't it. The material was stiffened," explained Ms. Futuro. "On a plaque attached to the ladder of the Lunar Module are these words:"

**'HERE MEN FROM THE PLANET EARTH
FIRST SET FOOT UPON THE MOON
JULY 1969, A.D.
WE CAME IN PEACE FOR ALL MANKIND'**

On the way back to the transport, Danny and Cathy stopped and looked around them. The others kept going. The moonscape was barren and lifeless. They leaned back and looked up at the stars. There, high above the gray rolling hills of the moon, against the blackest sky they ever saw, was the Earth, blue and green and white.

They stood and stared at it for a long time. Ms. Futuro did not disturb them. Cathy took out her notebook for the Kid's Guide to the Moon and wrote, "From the surface of the moon, Earth is beautiful. It looks very small and fragile. It reminds me of a marble."

GLOSSARY

Crater: A bowl shaped cavity. Craters are caused by the impact of a meteorite, micrometeorite, asteroid, or some other object.

Crescent Moon: The phase of the moon when it is seen as a sliver in the sky.

First Quarter: A quarter of the moon is visible to people on Earth one week after the New Moon.

Full Moon: The entire lighted side of the moon is visible to people on Earth two weeks after the New Moon. The moon looks round.

Gravity: A property that causes things to attract and to be attracted by all other things. Gravity causes matter to clump together. The gravity at the surface of the Earth is six times stronger than the surface gravity of the moon. Objects on the moon weigh one sixth what they do on Earth.

Last Quarter: A quarter of the moon is visible to people on Earth three weeks after the New Moon.

Maria: Lava-flooded plains on the moon that look like dark areas to people on Earth.

Matter: The substance things are made of. It can be a gas, liquid, or solid.

Micrometeor: A tiny particle of dust slowed down by Earth's atmosphere so that it floats to the surface of Earth. Also, micrometeorites are tiny particles traveling through the solar system at high speed. They hit planets, moons, asteroids, spacecraft, and other objects.

Meteorite: A meteor that reaches the surface of Earth or another body in the solar system.

NASA: National Aeronautics and Space Administration; the U.S. agency in charge of activities in space and space exploration.

New Moon: The lighted side of the moon is turned away from the Earth. The moon is invisible to people on Earth.

Orbit: The curved path of a planet, satellite, or other object around another object.

Solar Wind: A stream of high speed particles (pieces of atoms) flowing out from the sun through the solar system.